written by
NYASHA WILLIAMS

illustrated by
JADE ORLANDO

ALLY BABY CAN
BE ANTIRACIST

HARPER
An Imprint of HarperCollinsPublishers

Who can be antiracist?

ALLY BABY CAN!

Ally Baby makes a change when they take a stand!

Being an ally is what you do
and the actions you make commonplace.

Allies **SUPPORT** those treated unfairly because of things like race.

Race is how we look—
our skin color, eyes, and hair.
Race is a construct based on traits
that groups of people share.

THE FIVE CATEGORIES OF RACE IN THE UNITED STATES ARE:

- Black or African American
- American Indian or Alaska Native
- Asian
- Native Hawaiian or other Pacific Islander
- White

Racism is discrimination against a certain race.

UNFAIR HOU
PREDOMINAN
OVERPO
GENERA
WEA
UNEQUA
EDUCATION

NG & EMPLOYMENT

Y WHITE INSTITUTIONS

LICING

IONAL

TH GAP

Antiracism is the work we do
so injustice has no place!

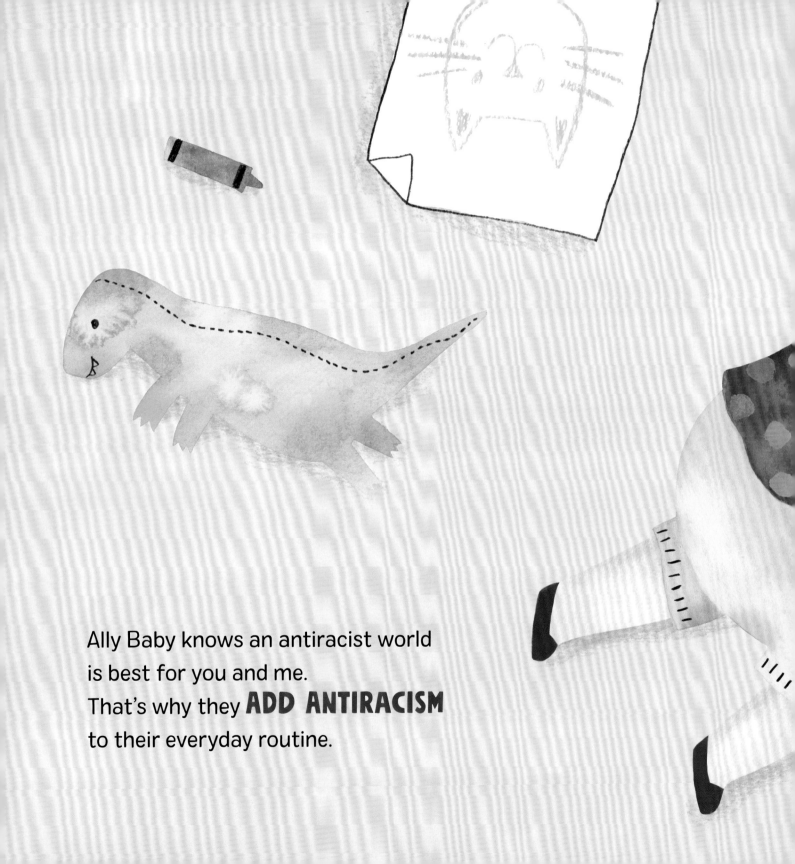

Ally Baby knows an antiracist world
is best for you and me.
That's why they **ADD ANTIRACISM**
to their everyday routine.

Ally Baby **LISTENS** to others
and knows when to speak up.

Ally Baby **CALLS OUT RACISM**,
even when it gets tough.

Your hair
is so **curly!**

STOP! Don't touch
Stella's hair.

Ally Baby puts in a big effort to **LEARN**, unlearn, and accept.

Ally Baby makes mistakes but
acknowledges, **APOLOGIZES**, and reflects.

BREAKFAST TIME!

pajeon

pupusas

grits

Ally Baby eats different foods homemade by their neighbors.

Ally Baby **EMBRACES** all cultures—
a first step toward changed behaviors!

kimchi

pampoenkoekies

maduros

Ally Baby **SPEAKS OUT** and refuses
to let a classmate be excluded.

Ally Baby **TAKES DAILY ACTION**
so that everyone is included.

PLAYTIME!

Ally Baby is not color-blind;
they **SEE** and celebrate all colors.

Ally Baby **DOESN'T JUDGE**
or make assumptions about others.

Ally Baby **MARCHES** loud
for the BIPOC community.

Ally Baby always **SHOWS UP**
to promote love and unity.

JUSTICE

EQUITY

Ally Baby **LEADS** the way—
stepping for equal chances and rights.

But Ally Baby **STEPS BACK** so friends can offer different insights.

Ally Baby **TALKS OPENLY** about what they hear on the news.

Ally Baby doesn't shy away
from heavy topics or others' views.

DINNERTIME!

Ally Baby **READS** many books
that star brand-new faces.

Ally Baby loves hearing stories
about people of all backgrounds and races.

Ally Baby yawns and stretches just before they close their eyes.

Ally Baby **DREAMS OF POLICY CHANGE** and the day that we all rise!

BEDTIME!

Ally Baby fully commits to the ally work they do.
Ally Baby CAN be antiracist and yes, friends,

SO CAN YOU!

Ally is more than a noun; it is a verb.
As an ally, you can take action against injustice when you:

ADVOCATE: Stand up in spaces where you can; use your privilege and access to resources to better serve those who are marginalized; and seize every opportunity to combat racist ideas and dismantle racist policy. S-u-p-p-o-r-t!

LEARN: Educate yourself, your family members, and your friends about different identities and experiences and about the history of racism.

LET GO: Challenge your own discomforts and prejudices by letting go of racist values. Let go of the need to be front and center; let BIPOC groups lead too.

YIELD RESULTS: Take action to create interpersonal, societal, and institutional change.

How was Ally Baby antiracist in this book?

ALLY BABY . . .

learned the definition of race and racism.

ate new foods with friends from different cultures and read stories featuring BIPOC characters.

discussed racial issues they saw in the news with an adult.

apologized when a BIPOC classmate called out their hurtful words.

made room for others to lead and be included in spaces like the playground and during the march.

did not stereotype others on the playground based on their race. Instead, everyone played together.

spoke up when others made racist comments about hair.

used their voice to protest racism.

redistributed new and valuable toys evenly so everyone had a chance to play.

What is one way you can be an antiracist ally today? How will you advocate, learn, let go, and yield results?

ALLY BABY'S FIRST WORDS

A vocabulary list for antiracist allies:

ALLY: a person who is not a member of a marginalized group but who supports that group. **Coconspirator** and **advocate** are other terms often used.

ANTIRACIST: a person who opposes racism and promotes racial equity and justice.

BIPOC: stands for Black, Indigenous, and People of Color.

COLOR-BLIND: the false belief that race does not affect a person's socially created opportunities.

CONSTRUCT: an accepted idea that has been created by the people in a society.

CULTURE: the customs, arts, social institutions, and achievements of a particular nation, people, or other social group.

DISCRIMINATION: unfair treatment of a person or group. In society, this can play out in laws, social interactions, and a nation's policy.

EQUITY: fairness or equality in the way people are governed and treated (also related: **social justice**, **equality**).

RACE: groups that humans are divided into based on physical traits regarded as common among people of shared ancestry.

RACISM: systems, ideas, laws, values, and structures that disadvantage certain racial groups and benefit others.

ALLY BABY'S READING LIST FOR ANTIRACISM

Antiracist Baby by Ibram X. Kendi

Woke Baby by Mahogany L. Browne

Our Skin by Megan Madison, Jessica Ralli, and Isabel Roxas

Let's Talk About Race by Julius Lester

A Is for Activist by Innosanto Nagara

10 Ideas to Overcome Racism by Eleonora Fornasari

The King of Kindergarten by Derrick Barnes

Eyes that Kiss in the Corners by Joanna Ho

Our Favorite Day of the Year by A. E. Ali

Kamala and Maya's Big Idea by Meena Harris

Hair Love by Matthew A. Cherry

Alma and How She Got Her Name by Juana Martinez-Neal

Laxmi's Mooch by Shelly Anand

Be Kind by Pat Zietlow Miller

ABOUT THE CREATORS

Photo by Kimberly Salas

NYASHA WILLIAMS is an author, educator, creator, and activist who works to decolonize literature, minds, and spiritual practices one day at a time. She is the author of the picture books *What's the Commotion in the Ocean?* and *I Affirm Me.* You can visit her at www.nyashawilliams.online.

Photo by Raven Shutley Studios

JADE ORLANDO was born on an army base in North Carolina and grew up in a tiny Michigan town. She is the illustrator of several works for children, including *Hey You!*, *Generation Brave*, and *Who Takes Care of You?* Jade currently lives in Atlanta, GA, with her husband, greyhound, and four cats (including two naked ones!) You can visit her at www.jadefrolics.com.

Ally Baby Can: Be Antiracist · Copyright © 2022 by HarperCollins Publishers · Written by Nyasha Williams · Illustrated by Jade Orlando · Special thanks to **Deonna Smith** and Luana Kay Horry · All rights reserved · Manufactured in Italy · No part of this book may be used or reproduced in any manner whatsoever without written permission except in the case of brief quotations embodied in critical articles and reviews · For information address HarperCollins Children's Books, a division of HarperCollins Publishers, 195 Broadway, New York, NY 10007 · www.harpercollinschildrens.com · Library of Congress Control Number: 2021948578 · ISBN 978-0-06-321453-8 · The artist used watercolor, Adobe Photoshop, and Procreate to create the digital illustrations for this book · Typography by Caitlin Stamper · 22 23 24 25 26 RTLO 10 9 8 7 6 5 4 3 2 1 ❖ First Edition